Nibbles

The Life Erotic: Part Two
A Discovery Journal

By Athena, writing as B. Unbidden

This work of fiction is intended for adult audiences. Names, places and events used are creations of the author's imagination and are purely coincidental.

Copyright © Athena
All rights reserved. No part of this product may be reproduced or used in any manner without the written permission of the publisher.

Second Edition Print 2023
ISBN: 978-1-960298-01-0 (print)
ISBN: 978-1-960298-04-1 (EPUB)

Published by Elder Glade Publishing, LLC
www.eldergladepublishing.com

Dedication

To all the delights of this
delectable world,

And all who relish upon them.

Enjoy your tastes, for you are
blessed to have them.

Monday: My Taste of Fear

Beloved, it's been too long since I've written. In all honesty, I've had some wine and may ramble on a bit. Not just any wine, a rich plummy red, a dark and mysterious blend. It reminds me of you, sweet on the lips, full and toned … and satisfying. I should stop, but it's so delicious I keep refilling my glass. If only you were closer, I'd keep filling myself with you instead.

B. Unbidden

It's been a strange set of seasons without you. I will take all the blame, of course. I left. It was my choice, my call, and I did not consult you once. I knew you'd talk me out of it. Knew you'd smile, or whisper, and I'd lose my resolve, so I crept away before dawn … breaking inside.

I was—am—a coward.

The intensity of your fire scared me. Your fearlessness terrified me. Your fierce hunger and feral beauty made me tremble—not for fear you'd hurt me, never that. But from fear that I would be blissfully consumed … unaware I was evaporating from the most exquisite heat. I feared I would be sucked into the insatiable bog of never having enough of you, that I would ruin you with my hunger.

In turn, I was afraid of being devoured. Happily so.

Afraid because I did not know what I would be giving up. How to explain to someone who has always known who and what they are?

How could I give myself to you in wild abandon, in blissful, riotous profusion, if I did not know myself well enough to understand what I was giving away? How would that have been fair to either of us?

I could have been gifting you my warmth, and it might have been my grief, mislabeled. I might have been granting you all my joy, but fringed with bitterness for all I had once relinquished, unwilling. I might have been sighing your name in the wonder of climax and feeling instead the last lover I'd never truly released.

How could I give you my unfettered self when I had no grasp of what I was holding on to. What challenges had I yet to taste. What simple joys had I yet to know by myself.

The truth, however difficult it was to admit to myself and thusly to you, is that I am not fully my own to give away … *yet.* I had not planned to fall in love, so when the time came to grant my heart, the secrets hidden therein were not yet mine to bestow.

I am ashamed for leaving without telling you where I was going. I hope someday you will begin to forgive me. In the meantime, I'll write these notes as much for myself and my discovery as for you—if you should care to read them. I don't know where I'll end up, but these notes are where I've been.

I have no right to tell you I miss you. I have no right to express how much I ache to be filled by you; by your body and your mind. I wish you joy and happiness, Beloved. I wish it with all my being.

Forgive me.

With love,
Blush

Tuesday:
Forbidden Fruit

It is said that if you announce your crime, your sin, or your weakness, absolution is a step closer and freedom lies within reach. It is said that if you name your fears and claim your demons, they no longer hold sway and you are soon released from the perdition of those yearnings that tempt and the terrors that bind.

I am Blush Unbidden, and I announce my crime as obstruction of my own gratification. My sin …

desire. My weakness … hunger. Freedom, I beg thee for mercy. My fear is asking, as I fear receiving all that I desire as much as I fear the withholding of satisfaction. Afraid to want, to ask, to need, and yet terrified of the hunger never being satiated.

And thusly, all named, I show you my demons, the tormentors of my sybaritic heart.

When I met my first lover, it was not the lover I expected, only because I knew not at the time lovers are amalgamates of stardust in a multitude of configurations—but that's a conversation for another day. No, this lover was a mango.

Yes, a mango.

It was the summer my sister and I flew to the West Coast to visit our father in California, four days past my twelfth birthday. I baked in the heat of the California sun, sweating, a halo of curls around my forehead.

My father pulled over at a fruit stand to rest. As I stepped out, a puff of dry earth settled across my sandaled toes. I wandered to the wooden stands under the shaded canopy to hide my pale skin from the sun. The last thing I wanted before starting middle school was a new wash of freckles. Mother wouldn't be pleased if I came home with a tan and new spots.

As I loitered near the edge of the tent, my father and sister gathered the familiar fruits. The wooden racks under the awning held a fruit I didn't recognize. Large oblong bursts of color. A deep rouge blending into an orange-gold hue on one side. I picked it up and found the weight odd. It was heavier than an apple, and smooth.

A boy my age with sun-darkened skin approached from around the corner. "You want the mango in the box?" His hair was black and dusty; his eyes bright with caged mischief.

I glanced at my father, who called out, "Mangoes! Yes, we'll take a dozen." Then he called to me, "Try one, Minnow. They're delicious." As he turned back to his other selections, I stared down at the beautiful fruit in my hand.

I lifted it to my mouth, prepared to take a full bite; the boy laughed. "Wait! You have to peel it first!"

Before I could puzzle out whether I was offended he'd laughed or relieved that he'd warned me, he pulled a knife from his pocket and reached for the mango. His fast, brown fingers took the fruit and expertly slid the knife across the ruby curve. A long sliver of skin fell to the dust, revealing golden flesh.

Juice spilled across his fingers as he took a second pass with the blade, picking up a thick piece of golden meat. "Here." He lifted the knife toward me, balancing the juicy bite.

I hesitated.

"It's good," he assured.

I took the slippery piece in my fingers and sniffed it. A warm, luscious scent. For years after, the smell of sun-warmed mangoes always brought me to the moment on the side of a California highway when I bit into a mango slice for the first time.

It slid past my lips, a soft, sweet pulp … sunlight itself. Juice dribbled down my chin, onto my white sundress. All thoughts fled my mind. My tongue froze. I'd never tasted anything so delicious. I forgot to breathe for a moment.

A strange thing happened to my body. I felt weak and a little breathless. At the same moment, my mouth was alive with flavor. I reached out, clutching the canopy post.

"It's good!" The boy chuckled.

Before I could answer, he peeled another slice. The sensation didn't end with the one bite, it swelled, my voice tangled. I couldn't speak—only nod and smile when he asked if I wanted more.

More, yes, more. A tightness in my lower body and a pulsing, sugary glow through my limbs made me tingle with the hope of something new and wonderful still to come.

My father had finished his selection. My sister honked the horn. I startled back to reality. For a moment I'd felt far away, lit within by honied radiance. I grinned and wiped my chin.

We shared a knowing glance, the boy and I. He'd opened a door to something, a glimpse of light. I wasn't sure what it was, but I smiled and thanked him. My father paid, and we were on our way to the car when I looked back.

The boy wiped his knife on his pants, then folded it and slipped it in his pocket. He offered a quick wave before disappearing around the side of a nearby stall.

I stared out the window as we drove, wondering why I'd never tasted a mango before. Was it a "forbidden fruit," as my mother would have called it, because it made me feel … something?

I heard her voice in my head. "All pleasures are forbidden. Lust is the downfall, the ruination of humanity. Lust for sex. Lust for money … it all paves the way straight to hell."

As I leaned against the car door, the warm California wind in my hair and a throbbing promise in my body I'd never before known, I began to wonder what other lusts could exist. Could one lust for mangoes? Could one go to hell for a fruit?

I was twelve the first time I masturbated. That night, after the fruit stand, I sat in my father's great bathtub while my family went to the movies. I soaked in the warm water, a dish of mango slices on the tub beside me while I touched myself and thought of the boy at the fruit stand.

I imagined his easy smile, his slick, juicy fingers, and reached my first climax.

It was so shocking, so overwhelming, so spectacular, that it terrified me. I was instantly filled with shame. I imagined everyone had heard me, miles away, and that my mother would know, somehow. She would just know.

I didn't touch myself for two more years. And I didn't eat mangoes again until high school, when Adelle Shapiro brought mangoes to class and we snuck back to the empty hall by the auditorium to eat them and tell each other secrets … but that's another story.

The point is, Beloved, that deep within my hidden yearnings, there always lay a fissure of fear. Fear of such power over my body and its wants. Fear that my hunger, curiosity, and lust would damn me in some way, or worse … damn those I love.

To be completely *unbidden*, I must know the depths of this shame, this fear, and undo it. It no longer serves my desires to be bound by such terrors. If I am ever to give over to you completely, I must free myself of these old fears.

It started with a fruit ... but it didn't end there. The delights of a sybarite are never-ending.

Wednesday:
Passport in a Bottle

I was invited to a party my sopho-more year of college. It was supposed to be a wild affair out at the beach, with music, drinking … and boys. My friend Amelia convinced me to go, promising my mother would never hear about it.

I took extra care dressing and went through considerable effort to straighten my curls and appear fash-ionably coifed. I wore red nail polish and matching panties ... certain that, in the evening, that fact might become relevant.

By no means was I virginal, having relinquished that burden years earlier with much satisfaction. But that's another story ...

The truth was, I was freshly single and looking forward to being out and about, to be seen having fun. No moping heartbreak, no sense of being sullied by the tar of rejection. Revenge partying? Perhaps.

The beach was packed with students. The sun had set, and music hammered from speakers in the back of a truck. Amelia quickly met up with the boy she'd been eyeing all semester. I was happy for her. She was glowing with excitement, her round face alight with the early stages of love.

The party was loud. A guy from the football team pressed a wine cooler into my hand, then tried to chat me up with a vapid, "Hey, girl."

I suddenly felt very lonely.

My plans of being seen felt foolish and small. The crowd was loud and obnoxious. The music was so dissonant that I couldn't hear myself think, much less understand the sad attempts at conversation from the football player pushing a second drink into my other hand. I mumbled, "Thanks, but I only have two hands."

"Drink faster," he retorted. "I'll be back with more." He disappeared into the crowd, toward the keg.

I quickly made my escape. I wandered to the edge of the event, where sea grass tufted on the dunes and the light from the party stopped and starlight began. There were a few scattered bodies along the beach, couples having sex or making out. I slipped by them … envious.

I walked along the surf until I couldn't hear the music, lost in my thoughts.

"Are you running away from it too?" a deep voice asked.

I flinched and spun around. I hadn't seen him as I walked by. He was a shadow lounging against a driftwood log. A cherry light blossomed, and as he exhaled I smelled tobacco.

"I thought I wanted a party … but I guess not," I mumbled.

The shadow chuckled and said, "Yeah, I didn't want to come, but I was wingman so I couldn't skip." He lifted a bottle. "Want a drink?"

The starlight was enough to see his outline, but not his face, so I stepped toward him. "Thanks, but I'm good." I lifted my wine cooler, though I hadn't even had a sip and didn't know what flavor it was.

He stood and I had the sense he was taller than me. "I see. Well, that is a drink, to be sure. I should re-phrase … would you like something better to drink?"

I bristled.

"Not that wine coolers don't have a place in this world, but this … this is a single malt Scotch."

The scent of cigar wafted on the

sea breeze as he walked toward me. I tucked my sweater closer. Then he was near enough I could see his features. He was lovely, in a square-jawed sort of way. With shaggy, curly hair and a cleft chin.

"Drinking a single malt is like tasting a different world. It's not what you drink to get drunk … drunk drinking is for the kiddies. This …." He raised the bottle so I could see it in the starlight. "This is what you sip to taste the moment, to savor … it's …." He pondered his last words as he sucked on his cigar, then finished as he exhaled. "It's about the senses."

Senses. Yes. That was what I wanted.

"Yes, please," I said, and smiled. My lower belly uncoiled and pulsed.

"Here, let me get rid of that for you." He took the wine cooler from my fingers and propped it on the sand. "Please join me out here on the fringes while our cohorts obliterate their dignity elsewhere. Yeah?"

I laughed. "Sure."

"I'm Brian."

"Blush."

I followed him back to the log, where he retrieved a duffel bag. He quickly built a small fire from driftwood and some paper. I settled into the sand beside him and held his cigar while he worked.

"Go ahead, try it," he encouraged. "Suck it into your mouth and hold it on your tongue, but don't inhale. If you inhale, it will make you sick at first." He winked. "Just taste."

I'd tried to smoke once or twice, but it always ended in coughing fits and discomfort. So, it never stuck. But I was curious, and afraid to disappoint, so I did as he instructed and held the smoke on my tongue.

"Can you taste the sweetness in the smoke?"

I coughed a little, and in the exhale tasted the sweetness he mentioned. I liked it. "Yes."

He smiled, and I couldn't help but reciprocate for how charming his lips were. The small fire illuminated his features, and I thought again how oddly lovely he was. No longer a boy, but not quite verging on a man. He was youthful and warm, with a tangible charisma.

When he held the bottle out, he asked, "Have you had Scotch before?"

I shook my head.

"Okay, well, it's strong, so start small. Just hold a little in your mouth and let the flavors open to you." He scooted closer. "The flavors will tell you a story if you let them."

I gingerly took the bottle and held it to my lips. A little sip. Held it on my tongue.

It was powerful. Bold. Shocking. In a panic I swallowed, and the acid burn of alcohol slid all the way to my belly. I coughed.

Brian laughed. A warm, inclusive chuckle. "Whoa. See? It's strong the first time. If I had a proper glass and one ice cube, I could help the taste open more."

"It wasn't awful," I said, grinning. "After the burning, I thought I tasted …" I swallowed again and pondered my words. "I thought it tasted like woodsmoke."

"Yes!" Brian chirped. "But that's only part of the story. There's so much more to it. There are wind-swept cliffs along the sea, and thunder rolling across the Scottish countryside, and …"

I caught his excitement; hungering for the story he was telling, wanting to know what he knew. Wanting his hands on me, his lips and breath against my body.

"Show me," I whispered, leaning in.

He stammered, paused, and stared at me. He didn't look at me like the football player–frat boy trying to get me drunk enough to take advantage. He didn't look at me like my literature professor, a hungry lion behind a plexiglass wall. He didn't look at me like anyone had ever looked at me before.

He looked at *me*.

Then he wordlessly reached out, pulling my body closer, helping me up onto his lap, where I straddled his legs. "Let me show you?" he asked reverently. "Take you to Scotland in this bottle?"

I nodded, even as my heart hammered against my sweater buttons. I smiled. He smiled. Then he took a long sip from the bottle and planted it in the sand. When he reached both hands for my face, I felt weak and light.

His fingers slipped through my hair as he pulled me into his kiss. Scotch dribbled down our chins as his lips met mine. My mouth was full of his tongue and the tang of iodine from sea-washed barrels and brined malt. My legs tightened around him as I swallowed his mouthful of peat-smoked saliva and inhaled his caramelized breath.

More. I want more. I paused to gasp for breath, to kiss his neck, to tangle my fingers in his hair. He took another swig and we were spiced with a hint of peppery cinnamon, warmed with sun and a brassy base note of candied orange.

We stopped, breathless and panting. The front of my sweater was soaked. My throat, drenched. He reached up, carefully unhooking my buttons, pausing at each loop to make eye contact, asking softly, "May I?"

I smiled and kissed his nose at each pause.

"What did you taste?" he whispered.

"Caramel." I gasped as his lips pressed full upon the bared hollow of my Scotch-soaked cleavage.

"And …?" he prompted.

"Lemon?"

He kissed my skin and skimmed his fingers over the clasp of my bra. "Citrus. Oranges."

My bra slipped off and I sat straddling his lap, topless, the gleam of alcohol glistening on my pale skin in the firelight.

"Spice."

"Yes," he murmured as he picked up the bottle. "Cinnamon," he finished, taking a hearty swig. Then he captured my right nipple in his warm, single-malt lips.

And so our undressing went. I reciprocated, sipping and kissing his flesh as I worked his shirt over his head. We were naked, sticky with drink, covered in sand, and feverish with need, when he put his mouth to me and tongued me across the Scottish countryside. There was a slight sting from the alcohol on his breath, but then the grip of his fingers on my thighs and the surge of heat through my lower lips made me buck and beg for more.

Then, in climax, I felt him clutch me tight, holding me safely in his grip as I trembled and shook, gasping. When I surfaced, a break I didn't know I needed from the tension left me grinning, panting.

"My turn?" I whispered when I could speak.

"You don't have to," he said.

"I know," I agreed. "But I'm not done tasting …" I squirmed about and wriggled to where I could press him back against the sand. The small fire was dying to embers as I gazed upon his beautiful face.

The bottle was nearly empty, though we'd swallowed very little of it. I filled my mouth, kissed him, then bent to lick his engorged cock. He gasped and flexed.

"Caramel again," I said, and licked. As I exhaled, the vanilla notes surfaced. "And sweet." I licked. "And smoked peat." I licked. I swigged again. "Band-Aids?"

"Iodine," he corrected in a strangled voice, clutching fistfuls of sand, breathing deep. "Iodine from the seawater and brine."

I licked again. With each stroke, I echoed the motion with my hand around his cock, until I ran out of new flavors from the Scotch and leaned in to kiss him and drive him over the brink with my fingers.

He came on my breasts in hot, spurting waves and a wordless shout. I smiled and kissed his grin as he broke out into a loud post-orgasm laugh and pulled me hard against him. We were a mess. Sticky, sandy, and spent.

I'd lost track of time. As I collapsed

on his shoulder and we stared up at the sky, I thought I heard my name being called. A frantic voice in the distance.

I sat up. "Amelia! I completely forgot."

He was a gentleman, helping me scramble through the sand, looking for my clothes. I found my bra and skirt, my sweater and sandals, but I couldn't find my panties.

"They match my nail polish, they can't be hard to find!"

"Blush!"

"Just a minute!" I called back. "Over here. Give me a minute."

Brian began laughing heartily when Amelia stepped over the small sand dune, with her new flame, and saw me working the buttons on my sweater.

"Rod?" Brian laughed.

Amelia and Rod held hands. Rod looked back and forth, from me to Brian, then said, "Gold star, wing-man. Gold star."

"Oh, shut up," Amelia hissed, breaking away from him. "You okay, Blush?"

I nodded. "More than okay." I glanced at Brian and smiled. "I think I've fallen hard for a new kind of drink."

Something shifted that night. I could no longer pretend to enjoy parties with no sense or sensory anchor. I could no longer pretend conversation with people who wished only to talk about the weather. It was all I could do to politely decline the next foisted wine cooler without a terse quip, because I had been introduced to a new way to experience flavor. The story of the flavor, the action of the flavor. I had glimpsed something much more delicious, and I was hungry for more.

The sybaritic lust for experience grew within. The small trip to Scotland through the lips of a partner was all the encouragement I needed to begin looking for new adventures, flavors, and encounters.

P.S. Brian and I dated briefly, but remained friends for years. Nearly a decade later, he sent me a package with a note: "I went back the next morning looking for them. I confess, I kept them for a few years, hanging in my Scotch cabinet to remind me of you, your scent and taste and that

sexy nail polish. But I'm getting mar-
ried now, and it seems the right time
to return these to their proper owner.
Thank you for that amazing night."
My red-lace panties were enclosed.

Thursday: Bittersweet Beginnings

It was my lit professor who first gave a name to what I am. Sybarite. Our story is strange and complicated, but I should first state that he never coerced me or advanced beyond what I offered or invited.

I'd had Professor Levine for an unprecedented three semesters. No matter which class I registered for, I found myself shuffled into his lectures halls and classrooms. Though he gazed at me as if he had not eaten in days, he never once approached me unprofessionally. In retrospect, I realize he was waiting patiently for two years; a lion in the grass, hunting.

My papers were always returned with questions to my questions. When I compared my marked work with other students in his class, their graded comments were perfunctory and short. My notes from him were in black ink, and thoughtful. Theirs were in red.

It didn't escape my notice that he corrected my work with a different pen and a different eye. Despite my odd favoritism, I only netted passing grades from him. A colossal disappointment to my hopes of becoming a writer.

For the two years I was in his college classes, I thought him a normal-looking man. He was so average, he could have set the very description of the term. Not quite six feet tall, brown hair, mid-forties, with an extra ten or so pounds. He was always clean-shaven and wore light-rimmed glasses. I guess what I'm trying to say is, I would not have been able to pick him out of a crowd. Yet during the two years we spent together after, I discovered I could see only his face, pick out only his scent, hear only his voice … even in a packed theater.

He made his move the day I graduated.

When he approached to con-gratulate me, he handed me a small envelope and a box. The warm wind ruffled my gown. I accepted the gift, believing it strange that he'd made the effort.

"Congratulations, Blush," he said.

"Thank you, Professor Levine," I replied.

"This is for you." He paused and waited for me to take the package before continuing. "I've been waiting for a chance to tell you that you're a very beautiful woman."

My face heated. I glanced away.

"Anyway," he went on, "I recognize the soul of the sybarite in you, from one to another."

I looked up. "Sybarite?"

"It's all in there," he said, pointing at the box. "I'd like to continue teaching you." He smiled and added, "Not literature and writing, but something else. If you're interested."

"Like what?"

He smiled. I noted the fine lines around his eyes crinkled, and the early signs of gray in his right temple. "Enjoy your day, Blush. You've earned it. Then, when you have time, explore the package." He stretched out a hand. I shook it as he finished. "If the gift makes sense to you, my number is inside."

He left me on the lawn by the steps. He did not glance back, blending effortlessly into the milling bodies.

Once home, I unwrapped his package: a small black book bound in glossy leather, and a box of chocolates with a manufacturer's label I didn't recognize.

His note read:

Dearest Blush,

I see the sybarite in you. We learn to recognize one another. Your curiosity gave you away. Your hunger to understand larger questions, to discover answers, to know and experience and write about it.

As I am no longer your professor, I can freely tell you that curiosity, that thirst to understand, makes me ache to teach you more, if you will have me.

A sybarite is an explorer. We stretch, reach, and yearn for delight, for knowledge, for answers, for experiences and sensory wonders. We never stop tasting. We never stop feeling. We are always tuned to the world and the elixir of living in a human form. We seek pleasure, challenge, and release.

This box of chocolates is made by a sybaritic chocolatier who understands our tastes—the heightened, the hungry, the decadent … the forbidden. If you want to know more about yourself and what you can do, eat these chocolates blindfolded. Taste them while you lie in the dark, feeling the texture with your tongue, the juices with your mind and body. Then write about it in the enclosed journal. You're a good writer. This journal will help you capture your feelings and sharpen your skills.

If the experience is for you what I believe it will be, and you want to know more of what you are capable of doing, of where a sybaritic spirit can lead … call me when you're ready.

Deliciously,
Donald

I puzzled over the letter and the box of chocolates for hours. His words strummed a chord I'd been unable to express for years. Just his words. Just the naming of the constant hunger I'd always known. Sybarite. The ache of never being satiated, never understood, never having enough information or enough flavor. *More, yes. More.*

"We seek pleasure, challenge, and release."

And yet, because his letter had stirred so much longing in me for an answer to years of aching, I feared the box of chocolates. Feared it like nothing before. I stared at it, sitting on the table, as though it were a package of spiders. I paced, hands shaking. I chewed my lip and paced still more, until his words stopped looping in my head and the resulting curiosity overcame my fear.

At last, when I worked up the courage to open the box of candy, it was not what I expected. Inside were four chocolates with labels.

The top note read: "From light to dark, blindfolded."

The lightest chocolate was long and slender, nearly the size of my thumb. The label above it read: Lovers' First Kiss.

The remaining three chocolates were: Sybaritic Heart, Underworld Bound, and Risen Flame.

They say curiosity killed the cat. Who says it? I wonder. Certainly not the cat. For if I happened to be said feline, I would say it was not the curiosity that did me in but the fear of living a life without answers, which would be a much more terrible fate than any death curiosity could conjure.

I positioned the box on my nightstand, to reach it in the dark. I stripped naked and blindfolded myself, then fumbled to the bed and lay down in the dark, heart hammering. Possible answers lay just beyond the veil. I trembled.

I bit into Lovers' First Kiss. Liquid filled my mouth. The milk chocolate gave way to puréed cherries soaked in brandy, with a heavy sugared cream. I smiled and tasted. Lovers' First Kiss hinted at early passions, at sweet, innocent chemistry. It tasted of hopeful longings and fruity wanting.

As I swallowed, it reminded me of desperate fumbling with unfamiliar clothing, and the delicious lips of my first love.

How strange a chocolate could capture the flavor of that memory so well, evoking the recall of my first night with the boy I'd fallen in love with. We'd tangled together, slippery in the summer heat. Sweating and kissing, sliding in and out of one another, exploring away the innocence. Lovers' First Kiss was perfectly named. I swallowed eagerly and reached for Sybaritic Heart.

The chocolate was darker, earthier. My teeth cut into a caramel center, and my mouth filled with a salted, brown-sugar candy with hints of lavender and cream. I rolled it around my tongue, extracting every sleek and gooey texture, marveling at the balance of sea salt, sugar, and lavender, as though I sat in a seaside garden … indulging in a treat that brought fresh dew to my inner thighs.

My hips moved, and my hand slipped down my breasts.

As I swallowed, warmth built in my belly. My clit throbbed. I could almost see my lover-to-be on the fringes of my mind's eye. Hunger bucked my hips, a need for more.

I reached for Underworld Bound. Bitter dark chocolate coated a black licorice middle, and deep inside that dark, tarry lust was a nugget of candied ginger. It was awful, then amazing, then mystifying. Yet I chewed, tasted, and blended the cryptic flavors in my mouth. As saliva moved the flavors around, marrying the textures and tastes, a warm, glowing essence emerged. What once tasted foul became an exotic piquancy.

My hips bucked, and my skin flushed. Heat swelled my nipples, and the rush of flavors left my lips as a musky, mysterious scent encapsulated in a moan.

What witchery or magic did the chocolates have? Drugs, maybe? Did it matter? Not really.

My fingers slipped down my belly and between my legs. The shadowy visual of my lover-to-be crystalized in my mind.

Professor Levine.

I gasped as I imagined his clean-shaven face and brown hair between my thighs. I imagined him tasting my cleft, and that it tasted like ginger and chocolate laced with black licorice. My breath labored. I panted in building ecstasy until I climaxed, lurching up, nipples taut, spasming to the fiction of his tongue and fingers driving me to an exotic, flavorful release.

I flopped back, adjusting my blindfold, grinning and panting.

Then I reached for Risen Flame. The black, bitter chocolate covered a creamy spicy center. Sun and red chilis, nutmeg, and cinnamon, played across my lips. I moaned, savoring the decadence of promise yet to be fulfilled, a hint of depths to be plundered, of the suggestion that there was yet another veil to cross ...

another threshold to be discovered and challenged.

Risen Flame teased a possibility beyond a place my imagination had ever gone, to a threshold of pleasure I'd never reached.

My post-orgasm glow lit up with the heat from the spiced chocolate. My muscles relaxed, and my pulse beat strong. As I swallowed, my body felt like I'd consumed a star. Warmth flowed through my limbs, rippling down my legs. My orgasm had built not as a thunderclap, but as a sensuous, tender lover. The heat spread under my skin, my body hummed from such radiant longings, and I sighed, surrendering.

I shuddered and gasped as I imagined my lover, his mouth on my nipples, drinking sunlight from my breasts, and his body sliding into mine, coaxing. My climax was a release from a deep place I rarely allowed. A shameful space within my mind filled with hungry needs and sinful yearnings. I opened to it, to him, to the taste and desire as my long, rolling climax surged through the breakers and into a violent release.

I lay in the dark, quivering, chocolate and spice on my breath, replete.

We seek pleasure, challenge, and release.

I thought I felt his hands on my body, caressing the last of my tremors free from the long-contained prison of my fears. At last, as my skin cooled, and the flavors left my tongue, I pulled my blindfold off and stared at the ceiling.

The chocolates had hinted, luring me with the idea that there was more to come, more story, more tastes, more. The flavor journey from innocent hunger to dark yearnings and release made me realize ... if there was a sybaritic chocolatier out there who understood how to capture that journey in the delicacies of a box of candy, to evoke orgasm through flavors and imaginings—what else could sybarites do?

My body hummed, sated for the moment. Yet, I feared once the taste had been given, and the reward found so gratifying, I would be hungry again soon ... for more.

I rolled over, naked and quivering … and picked up the phone.

If curiosity killed the cat, I hoped I would be so lucky as to die with such a satisfied smile on my face.

Friday: Elementals

Professor Levine chose the restaurant; an intimate space with a warm fire and large glass windows. We took a table by the windows near the street.

It was all a bit uncomfortable at first. I met his large brown eyes and soft round face and found I had no words beyond the perfunctory courtesies. He was polite, mannerly. My heart thundered with uncertainty and my belly clenched with the hunger of so many questions I was too afraid to ask.

As the server brought the wine menu, I snuck a peek at the man I'd taken classes from for two years. He was suddenly a very different face; as though I hadn't truly looked at him before.

"Do you mind if I do the ordering?" he asked me.

I shook my head, words stuck in my throat. As he scanned the menu, I took in his well-trimmed haircut and clean hands. He was a scholar, a man of books.

"This bottle," he said to the waiter and pointed. "Please don't say the name as it will be a surprise."

The server nodded and left.

"You're strangely quiet, Blush," he said in a teasing tone.

"I'm not sure where to start," I murmured.

"Ah." He smiled. "I felt the same when I was first awakened."

"Awakened?"

He nodded and splayed his napkin across his knee. "The naming of desires, the shelter of acceptance, the courage to begin exploring." He looked at me. "It's all part of what we call the awakening."

I smiled. "Oh."

"If we are very lucky, in this lifetime, we may have many awakenings. Layers upon layers of opening."

I picked up my water, hand trembling slightly. "Oh." As I sipped, he met my gaze.

"Did the chocolates speak to you?"

I nodded. "Very much so." Heat rushed up my neck; my cheeks flamed. "Thank you."

"Good." He smiled. "It's my pleasure to steer a bud toward the path, as I was guided in my beginning." He blinked. "Perhaps one day, you'll help another out of the bog in return."

The server returned with a bottle of merlot, a label I didn't recognize. The nearby firelight reflected off the deep burgundy pour. When he left us alone, Donald said, "It's easy to overwhelm in the beginning, so we should start with a few guidelines."

I nodded. Guidelines. That sounded prudent.

"Safe words will come later, but for now, I want you to be comfortable

with the words 'no' and 'stop.' Sybaritic life is about consent. The
moment you say or whisper or mut-
ter or sneeze those words—we stop.
Understand?"

I nodded again. "Yes."

"Secondly, when you are ready to
walk away from me or this instruction, do not ask for permission. It is
not mine to grant. You never owe ex-
planations or excuses. You are a free,
powerful woman. From this moment
forward, I release you, so you never
need to say goodbye. When you're
done, you will know it, and I will
wish you well upon your journey." He
chuckled. "You will learn eventually,
but woe be unto anyone who dares
try to entrap a sybarite unwilling."

His words were so strange. A

concept I'd never pondered before. Absolute freedom and autonomy in the engagement and presence of exploration.

"I understand," I whispered.

"More on those some other time, I suppose." He grinned and lifted his glass. "Want to play a little?"

I smiled. "Yes, please."

My first instruction at the hand of a fellow explorer was simple. In fact, I didn't realize the depth of the lesson until much later, lying in bed. As I pondered that simple glass of wine, and bright company, I realized the tutoring was sensory, but more so it was about willingness and active restraint.

Restraint.

"Tell me what you smell in this wine. Just the scent," he began.

I swirled my wine in the glass, admiring the color, and imagined it would make a lovely shade for a gown. When I inhaled the aroma, I was immediately brought to sun-drenched rows of bright autumn grapes. I closed my eyes and savored the scent.

"Sunlight. Sweet cherries. Black-berries. Almonds?"

"I can pick out the almonds, too." He agreed when he sniffed the glass. "What else?"

"Plum?"

"What else?"

"I don't … I can't smell anything else," I said, feeling as though I was failing an important test. I opened my eyes and glanced at the fireplace.

"There is no right or wrong answer, Blush," he said softly. "Only the depths of dipping into your curiosity, your hunger, and the ability to articulate what you find." He smiled encouragingly. "Try a sip."

I closed my eyes and sipped. It was a tangy merlot, full-bodied, rich in flavor and fruit.

"What do you taste?"

"I taste the cherries again, and earth, and blackberries."

"Good," he whispered, his voice close. "Now, as if this glass of wine is a lover, a mysterious puzzle you long to solve, sip again, and unravel your lover on your tongue."

I opened my eyes. He had moved

his chair closer to mine, his face earnest.

I blinked, took a breath, closed my eyes, and sipped again.

As though a lover I wished to unravel.

At first, I could only taste what I'd tasted before, but then, under all the other notes, a hint of metallic tang.

"Rust?" I said.

"Oxidation," he offered. "What else?"

I sipped, and when my mind opened up to the idea of metallic oxidation on my tongue, a sudden surge of flavors overwhelmed. "I taste sun and earthy rain," I murmured, surprised. "I taste honey from the bees … and something else."

"Yes!" he cheered softly. "Take it down to the elements if you can."

"Can I get you anything else?" the server asked from my left.

I jumped, startled, heart hammering as though I'd just been discovered doing something obscene in public.

I blushed, unbidden.

"We're fine, thank you," Donald said politely. Then he saw my face and chuckled. "You look like you got caught naked in public."

"Didn't I just, though?"

"In a manner of speaking, I suppose." He smiled and touched my arm. "Do you see where I'm going with this exercise?"

I shook my head. "Not yet."

"There is eroticism in all our endeavors as sybarites. Vulnerability, curiosity, hunger, the devouring of knowledge. It's all there, in what we eat, how we dress, which conversations we engage in … whom we love." He shrugged. "What I'm trying to say is, to be a sybarite is a way of living. A way of breathing and interacting with the world, and with our lovers."

I considered what he said. A lifetime of otherness was beginning to make sense. Not everyone was as hungry for answers as I was, and it often separated me from them as if I sat behind a fragile, clear barrier.

"When you allow yourself to live deeply in all that you do; to love deeply, to thirst deeply, and to explore all options down to the base elements, you'll begin to live in this world differently."

"But what if that pushes people

away?" I wondered, knowing that it would, had already done so.

"It will. Without a doubt it will frighten people near you, and they'll reject the way you live."

I sighed and nodded. "I know."

He offered a compassionate frown. "What else do you taste?"

I sipped and reached my senses into the wine as though it were my lover. After a time, the oddness of a taste I couldn't identify surfaced. "Loneliness."

"Ah, yes," he whispered, and took my hands in his own.

I opened my eyes, confused. "Loneliness has a flavor?"

He smiled softly and said, "Everything you explore, everything you taste and name and devour is a direct reflection of you, Blush." He caressed my cheek. "Because it is the way you live, and will live by what you are, the terms and identifications you make at first will be the way you truly taste, smell, and see yourself."

"I don't understand."

"You taste loneliness because you are lonely. That reflection of self will change eventually, but it's the most difficult beginning for us all."

"All of us?"

"I tasted only regret and bitterness when I was first awakening. I'd sort through all the flavors to the final dreg … and there I would meet my-self at the bottom with regret."

I tangled my fingers through his. "How did you learn to taste around it? To not feel it anymore?"

He grinned. "By practicing on my lovers, then on myself."

He kissed me then, gently. His fingers grazed my chin and smoothed my neck. When he pulled back, my skin hummed and lightning raced down my legs.

"Kiss me, Blush, and taste me all the way to the elements. Know that what you find at first is a reflection of yourself, then taste beyond it if you can."

The clink of diners' silverware faded. The heat from the fireplace dimmed. The room was suddenly a vacuum as my mouth reached for his, and my fingers slipped through his hair.

He was warm, and the merlot on his lips made me shiver into his touch. I leaned into his kiss and drank his tongue; the layers of his taste peeled away as I explored his mouth. I tasted past the stick of mint gum he'd used to freshen up, then discarded before he came into the restaurant. I tasted past his late afternoon coffee, all the way to the deep breath of city air he'd inhaled before walking into the building to meet me.

The more I tasted, the more I hungered. I clutched his shirt, pulling him into me as I drank past the flavors of his day into the dregs of his spirit. The tangy flush of pheromones in his mouth as he looked at me in my dress. The lusty edge to his need. The depth of his desire to help me open, and to be present when I bloomed.

And when I could go no deeper, I encountered the bitter acid of fear. Fear of rejection. It was such an unpleasant taste that I broke away, surprised.

I gasped, panting around the force of the kiss, and realized several people in the restaurant stared. Professor Levine panted, hair askew where I'd rubbed and pulled against him. "I'll ask for the check," he gasped.

I drew back. Stunned by my own public display and the heat in my lower body, vibrating to know more of him. My legs trembled as we stood.

I waited outside as he settled up. The misty rain was a welcome, cooling balm to the heat in my body—and the sour taste of fear.

When he walked out, he seemed

unbothered by the rain. "Thank you for a wonderful evening," he said. "May I walk you to your car?"

I blinked. He wasn't angling for an invitation to my place? Or offering? I was a little put out, as my body throbbed for him.

As if reading my thoughts, he said, "Slow and steady, Blush." He kissed my cheek and took my arm, leading toward the parking garage. "You know how to unravel the moment, to stretch out the exploration."

He helped me over the curb in my heels and tight dress. "But until you know which base tastes are yours and which belong to your lover … you'll never explore them fully, or yourself."

We stopped in front of my car. He waited for me to retrieve my keys.

"Thank you," I whispered. "I …" I ran out of words. "For the taste."

He leaned in and pecked my cheek. "Tasting, then pulling back and puzzling, then tasting some more … it's how we learn. Too much, too fast, and it brings out a darker, vampiric nature. There is a dark side to those like us, so it's best to start out softly."

I smiled and then looked away. "Just sips, then." I grinned. "Just nibbles."

"For now," he agreed.

Saturday: Taste of Longing

In all the explorations of my tastes, the nibbles and sips of life, the curious, the hungry, the desperate, there never was such a glorious flavor as you, Beloved.

Weeks have gone by without your salty cum on my tongue, your sweat-dampened skin on my lips. Weeks of thirst for your essence has left me barren and dehydrated. My fault. My choice, I know.

I wake in the midnight hours, clammy with dreams of our lovemaking. Yet my body is parched, cracking for the thirst of you. I lay awake, heart keeping time to the memory of blissful hips and thighs quivering with longing. I yearn with blinding agony for the sweet musk on your skin as I peck along your throat, and shiver into your deep moans.

I miss the fragrance of our desire, that spicy-sweet mix of cum and the metallic hint from a day of hard loving. I long for your off-key singing in the shower as you soap my body off your cock, then dance around the bedroom in your towel like you won the lottery before pecking me on the cheek on your way to pilfer the kitchen. *Lucky kitchen.*

I ache for that moment when you're pounding deep inside me as far as you can go while tumbling over the edge, unable to contain yourself any longer—living for that second when your eyes break focus and your muscles bind rigid. I come to life when the arch in your back flexes, and you lose yourself in my gaze; in that brief shatter I can't tell if you love me, or curse me, or both. But I drink you in, reveling in all that you are, rejoicing in that second of your pleasure so poignant it's painful—before you collapse in my embrace.

In those precious gasps, as you recover in my safety, I smooth your hair and give thanks to any god or goddess that blessed me with such a creature.

Then I remember I left. I walked away while you slept, unaware I was so furiously in love with you. Unaware that those silly things you do; the way you line your shoes up at the door just so, or that you forget your coffee in the microwave, or the way you point out every beautiful sunrise like it's the first one you've ever seen. I miss all of it. All of you.

I never told you with my lips, how much I love you. I trusted my eyes and body to sing your praise.

I should have told you.

I check my phone when I wake, panting from your absence. The night is black and empty without you so I scroll through photos of you, and burn with hunger. My need does not subside, and so I close my eyes and touch myself, and imagine your flavor.

Of late, that taste turns to the sour bile of the Underworld Bound, sybaritic dark chocolate coating a black licorice middle, and deep inside that dark tarry lust … a nugget of candied ginger.

Why? I wonder. Why can't I taste just you?

I know the answer. I'm not done here. My base elements reflect the flavor of a mystery I've kept even from myself. My exploration along the fringes of inner darkness are not settled. Until my darker sybaritic tastes have been fully explored and unraveled, my hunger for you can never be truly satisfied. I must confront that tarry place within, which I have feared to know.

Exploring that dark and hidden place may cost me all the trust and adoration you ever had for me.

I may lose you if I go deeper, but I will certainly lose us both if I do not.

Sunday Worship: Raspberries, Champagne, and Lust

Dearest Beloved,

As I sit down to my Sunday journal, I'm unable to express my longing. I have no right to tell you that your absence is a moonless night, but it's truth, so I speak it. The dawn I crept away from your sleeping form is the morning I most regret, even though I know it was a necessity.

In faith of you, I keep to myself. I have not shared my body with anyone else, only my memories. I have had teachers, partners, friends, lovers, loves … but only one beloved.

I share only my old stories, my histories, looking for a purge that will lead me to a place of brilliance, of clarity, and thusly back to you … if you are still free and will have me. If not, then I will be free of it all, though I would feel your loss deeply.

My sybaritic journey began with tastes, with the world explored through my tongue, but the body has many senses with which to feast, so my learnings did not stop at mangoes, chocolates, or wine.

Still, as I remember these stories of tastes, these little nibbles, I sit at my desk reminiscing fondly about that night you won the award and we came home in the early hours of morning.

I staggered up the stairs barefoot, carrying my heels and purse, laughing as you pulled me along, whispering what you would do to me if I lay down in the stairwell to sleep. We were still tipsy; the cab having left us on the curb, relieved we were getting out as we couldn't keep our hands off each other.

We stumbled into the condo, and I collapsed on the sofa. And you, Mr. Bigshot of the evening, pulled a fresh bottle of champagne from the fridge along with a dish of raspberries.

The scene was one of decadent sexual indulgence. You uncorked the champagne with a pop and filled our glasses with raspberries and sparkling, delicious champagne. You peeled my dress off as I unbuttoned you from your tux. What followed was a frenzy of wild, sexual abandon.

I tasted you all the way to your core. The effervescent glory of success, the sweet honey of long hours building mastery in your work, the rich molasses sugar of your desire for me. Then, below it all, a tiny sliver of metallic uncertainty.

The sun rose through the tall windows as I was splayed on the granite island, naked, covered in raspberry smears, and sticky with bubbly and cum. You leaned over me as I arched into you, our flesh bonding together with each stroke.

When you filled your mouth with sparkling wine and suckled my breasts,

I cried out with joy. And when I took your cock in my mouth and drank greedily of you … we sang into one another. Such notes and music only you have managed to draw from my lips.

Yet I wondered at that bitter taste of uncertainty … was it mine, or was it yours? That oxidized hint that not all was as it should be.

Sometime after we were both spent, you carried me to the bedroom. When we woke in the afternoon, we were stuck to the sheets, with raspberry seeds in my hair, and champagne kisses in my nether region that had left feathery tufts of the down comforter glued to my crotch. You stretched and groaned.

I smiled. "Good morning, Mr. Bigshot. I'm ready for your speech."

You chuckled and dragged my body toward you. "You smell like raspberries and sex."

"It's an expensive perfume," I said. "Only those who relinquish their dignity on the kitchen bar can afford it."

You chuckled again and rolled over, onto me. You caressed my face and gazed into my eyes. "Thank you for coming last night. It meant a lot that you were there."

I smiled, cupped your beautiful jaw, and kissed you. "I wouldn't have missed it for all the raspberries and champagne in the world."

And I meant it. Though the flush of that uncertainty rose all at once, and I realized that bitter metallic taste was not yours, but mine. The fear of the tarry, insatiable bog loomed, and I

worried I would break to have you—
or break you in the having.

I don't know how to get back to you sooner, Beloved. I don't know how to answer your worried texts and voice mails except to assure you … I will find a way to reach the space I must be in to give myself to you fully.

I go to the underworld, Beloved, to my deepest inner valley, to free myself from the darkening pitch. Then we can be together … if you will still have me. Please believe me when I say I go willingly, and with all my heart to discover these answers. I will find my way back to us, and when I do, I'll bring champagne and raspberries and prove how much I've missed you.

About the Author

Blush Unbidden is the nom de plume for an author of multiple works under various genres.

To B(e) Unbidden, is the freedom to dance, to live unfettered, enjoying the delicious abundance of love and life without restraint, without shame or judgment or recrimination. Only wild abandon along the sacred sexual journey of give and take, of grace and surrender, of falling deeply and uncontrollably in love with the vulnerability of being human.

Discover more B. Unbidden works at www.ElderGladePublishing.com.

To be continued in...

Blood of the Lamb

The Life Erotic: Part Three
A Discovery Journal

By Athena, writing as B. Unbidden

Price of Rubies

The Life Erotic: Part Four
A Discovery Journal

By Athena, writing as B. Unbidden

www.ingramcontent.com/pod-product-compliance
Lightning Source LLC
Chambersburg PA
CBHW061036050726
47592CB00004B/1460